Angela Som

the little Vampire

AND THE

MYSTERY PATIENT

Illustrated by Jon Miller

Translated by Sarah Gibson

SIMON & SCHUSTER
YOUNG BOOKS

Text copyright © 1989 C. Bertelsmann Verlag GmbH, Munich
Illustrations copyright © 1992 Jon Miller

First published in Germany in 1989
by C. Bertelsmann Verlag GmbH

First published in Great Britain in 1992
by Simon & Schuster Young Books

Photoset in 12pt Goudy Old Style in North Wales by
Derek Doyle & Associates, Mold, Clwyd.
Printed and bound in Great Britain by
The Guernsey Press Co. Ltd, Guernsey, Channel Islands

Simon & Schuster Young Books
Campus 400
Maylands Avenue
Hemel Hempstead HP2 7EZ

British Library Cataloguing in Publication Data available

ISBN 0 7500 1185 8
ISBN 0 7500 1186 6 (pbk)

Contents

The story so far...

Tony's best friends are Rudolph and Anna Sackville-Bagg, who are both vampires! Tony was given a tent and sleeping bag for Christmas, and the chance to go on an activity holiday of his choice. The vampires had been forced to leave the cemetery because of renovations by the nightwatchman, and they were living in an old ruined castle in the Vale of Doom. So, naturally, Tony asked his parents if he could go to the Vale of Doom for his holiday.

Tony met up with Rudolph and Anna at the spooky castle, but his holiday was cut short when his dad crushed his fingers in the old organ at the ruined chapel. Tony's parents thought that he was upset at having to leave the Vale of Doom so soon – but they didn't know that Tony's friends, the vampires, were also leaving, to return to their old vault in the cemetery!

This book is for Burghardt,
who shares all his secrets with me,
for Katja
and for all vampires, big and small.

Kidnapping

"Do I really have to go to the psychowotsit again?" asked Tony. He sat in the back of the car with a gloomy expression on his face.

"Yes!" His mother looked at him in the rear-view mirror and laughed – rather a forced laugh, Tony thought. Probably Mr Crustscrubber, the psychologist whom Tony was going to visit today, had advised her to try to keep in a good mood and not let anything upset her!

"I just don't see why I have to visit the psychowotsit!" grumbled Tony.

"He wants to have a little chat with you," replied his mother.

"A chat?" said Tony grimly. "Pump me with questions, interrogate me, squeeze the answers out of me, more like!"

"Oh Tony! You've been watching too many crime movies!"

"No I haven't, I haven't been watching enough!" retorted Tony, grinding his teeth. "Otherwise I would know what to do when . . . when someone kidnaps me!"

But instead of rising to this, his mother only laughed and asked, "What have you got against Mr Crustscrubber, anyway?"

"Nothing, nothing at all!" said Tony. "If he would just leave me in peace!"

"Now you're being unfair, Tony! After all, it was Mr Crustscrubber who had the idea of the activity holiday in the Vale of Doom. And you said yourself that you'd enjoyed the holiday – even though we had to come home a week early because of Dad injuring his hand."

"Well, I suppose so," admitted Tony. "The holiday was brill." *Thanks to Rudolph and Anna*, he added silently, but he kept that thought to himself.

"But that's just why I don't understand why I have to go and see Mr Crustscrubber," he said. "Especially now the holiday is over."

"Perhaps that's what he wants to talk to you about."

"About the holiday?" Tony was shocked. "Why should he?" Could his parents have somehow found out that Tony had met up with his best friends in the Vale of Doom – Rudolph Sackville-Bagg, the Little Vampire, and his sister Anna? Might they have shared their suspicions with Mr Crustscrubber? No! If his parents really had noticed something, they would have asked him about it immediately!

"Why are you always so suspicious?" asked Tony's mother. "Why not just wait and see what Mr Crustscrubber wants to discuss with you."

"Wait and see!" muttered Tony. "I bet *you* know exactly what he wants to see me for. You're bound to have rung him up!"

His mother laughed again. "No, it was Dad who telephoned. And if you really must know: Dad's been worrying about the holiday. After all, the holiday was your Christmas present, together with the tent and the sleeping-bag. And since the holiday ended up being only half as long as we'd planned because of all that business with Dad's injured hand, Dad thought you might have been . . . damaged mentally."

"Me? Damaged mentally?" Tony grinned to himself. "Well, I might have been," he said – in the hope of getting a couple of presents to make him feel better!

But at least now he was partly reassured as to what the visit to the psychologist was all about.

Cauliflower

"I would like to go in on my own," announced Tony, when his mother drew up in front of the large house in which Mr Crustscrubber held his practice.

"On your own? I don't know if that's a good idea."

"Do you think I might lose my way?"

"Well – you might go to that café over there instead of to Mr Crustscrubber!"

"No thanks," answered Tony, glancing contemptuously over at the café on the other side of the street. He had already been there once, after his first visit to the psychologist. "I don't like the ice-cream they have – and in any case, I haven't any money," he added, as a broad hint. But as he'd expected, his mother ignored it.

"All right then, if you've made up your mind to go in by yourself," she said, "I'll pick you up here in an hour."

"What?" exclaimed Tony. "Have I got to stay with the psychowotsit for that long?"

"Yes, that's the normal time for a consultation," answered Mum. And then, obviously conscience-stricken, she felt in her handbag after all and gave Tony fifty pence.

"Here," she said. "If you don't like their ice-cream, you can buy yourself a bun – but only *after* the consultation!"

"Thanks!" said Tony and took the money. He got out of the car with a grin and walked up to the house. A whole hour . . . he sighed.

Perhaps he should have taken Mum with him after all – at least she always had something to talk to Mr Crustscrubber about. The entrance hall smelled of cauliflower. Eeeugh! Tony shuddered and, to get away from the smell, he quickly rang the bell at the door with a sign on it which read:

GEOFFREY CRUSTSCRUBBER
Marriage Guidance Counsellor
and Child Therapist

Mrs Crustscrubber, a plump lady with an old-fashioned hairstyle, opened the door and said in a surprised voice, "Are you here already, Tony? Your appointment's not for half an hour . . . But come on in. You can go in the waiting room. We're just having our lunch," she added.

Tony went in, and at the same instant he knew what they were having for lunch: cauliflower . . .

He groaned quietly and, holding his breath, he followed Mrs Crustscrubber into the waiting room.

Save the Old Cemetery!

As soon as Mrs Crustscrubber had gone, Tony ran to the window and flung it wide open. Cauliflower! Tony would eat brussels sprouts, red cabbage, even spinach, without moaning – but cauliflower made his stomach turn!

His parents, who both thought cauliflower was particularly good for you, knew how he felt and only cooked it when Tony was out on a class expedition or something. Class expedition . . . As Tony leaned out of the window, drawing in deep breaths of air, he thought of what his teacher had announced that very morning with a beaming smile: that they would all be off on a trip to a residential school in the country in the autumn. There had been loud jubilation from everybody – everybody except Tony. If only he could persuade the Little Vampire to come along as well, it would certainly turn into a fun trip! But he was sure that Rudolph would not be at all interested in leaving his home in the vault again; after all, he and his family had only just returned to it from the ruins in the Vale of Doom.

The vampires had had to flee there because the nightwatchman of the cemetery, McRookery, and his assistant, Sniveller, had begun to "renovate" the old part of the cemetery, and in doing so had come menacingly close to the Sackville-Bagg family vault.

But now, of course, the building work had been stopped. Tony had heard all about it when he was staying in the Vale of Doom. The night before he left, he had been trying on an ancient suit with Anna in the cellar of the ruins, when all of a sudden Aunt Dorothy had popped up.

Tony had been able to escape from Aunt Dorothy by hiding in a large, black chest – and from inside the chest he had listened as Aunt Dorothy had reported that a petition by the townspeople to "Save the old Cemetery" had collected four hundred signatures against the renovation work.

By now the smell of cauliflower had disappeared, and Tony shivered at the wide-open window. He closed it again and went over to the low table in the middle of the waiting room, which was strewn with magazines and papers – probably advertisements for tranquillizers!

Tony's gaze fell casually on to one of these pieces of paper, and he nearly cried out loud in surprise: in thick, black letters was written "Save the Old Cemetery!" Trembling with excitement, Tony began to read:

Please help us preserve the old cemetery! Don't allow this, the most beautiful and oldest cemetery in our town, to be destroyed by raving fanatics!
Join the townspeople's campaign to Save our Old Cemetery. Help us with your signature!
For further information, please contact G. Crustscrubber, tel. 481218

When Tony had finished reading this appeal, he was so overwhelmed and confused he had to sit down.

"G. Crustscrubber" – was that the psychologist? Tony remembered seeing a telephone number on the brass plate by the front door. It had begun with a 48, he was sure of that. And Mr Crustscrubber's christian name was Geoffrey . . . Then suddenly, Tony remembered something else: back in the ruins, Aunt Dorothy had mentioned a "contact" whom she could telephone. When Anna had asked her who this contact was, she had simply answered in a riddle: "Scrub the bacon rind" and "dust the crust".

"Scrub the bacon rind," said Tony softly out aloud. "Rind . . . dust . . . scrub . . . crust . . . *Crustscrubber!*" he exclaimed. Aunt Dorothy's contact was Mr Crustscrubber! She must have come across one of his pieces of paper and dialled the number on it! Yes, that must have been what happened!

Tony read through the appeal once more.

"Please help us to preserve the old cemetery . . ."

Would it be a good idea to talk to Mr Crustscrubber about the petition, and to ask him for "further information"?

A Session with Mr Crustscrubber

At that moment, the door to the waiting room opened, and Mrs Crustscrubber looked in.

"We've finished lunch," she said. "My husband is waiting for you now."

Tony hastily folded up the piece of paper and stuck it in his trouser pocket. Then he got up and followed Mrs Crustscrubber through the hall, which still stank horribly of cauliflower. He coughed pointedly, and was relieved that Mr Crustscrubber's consulting room only smelled of ancient musty furniture.

Mr Crustscrubber was sitting behind a gigantic desk, the top of which was strewn with piles of books and pieces of paper. As Tony came in, he smiled at him in a friendly fashion, and pointed to the chair in front of the desk. Tony sat down. The untidiness of the desk and the fact that Mr Crustscrubber wore an old pullover and a pair of baggy cord trousers instead of a white coat had made Tony warm to him on his first visit – that is, as far as Tony was able to warm to any psychologist! But perhaps Mr Crustscrubber wasn't a typical psychologist at all. Tony recalled the extraordinary course of treatment

that Mr Crustscrubber had developed, which was supposed to help people suffering from particularly strong fears. Most of all, Mr Crustscrubber had wanted to try out this course on a vampire, but at the time, Tony had pretended he did not know any . . .

"Well, Tony, you're looking very thoughtful," said Mr Crustscrubber.

"Mmm, yes," said Tony.

"Are you thinking about your holiday?"

"About the holiday?" Tony hesitated. In actual fact, he had wanted to complain about the utterly useless Christmas presents – the tent and the sleeping-bag – which, after all, he had Mr Crustscrubber to thank for. But ever since he had read the piece of paper, his thoughts were spinning round the petition of the townspeople, and the part that Mr Crustscrubber had played in it.

"Did you enjoy the holiday?" asked Mr Crustscrubber, as Tony stayed silent.

"Well, yes . . . " said Tony and wondered how he could turn the conversation in the least obvious way from the holiday to "Save the Old Cemetery".

But it was more difficult than Tony had thought. Mr Crustscrubber seemed to take a burning interest in just about everything to do with the holiday in the Vale of Doom. Rather bluntly and with words of one syllable, Tony told him about what had happened and, since he naturally kept quiet about his escapades with the vampires, there was not all that much to tell. When he had finished, Mr Crustscrubber remarked that Tony seemed rather disappointed by the holiday.

"Disappointed?" repeated Tony.

If he didn't manage to start talking about the petition now, his hour would be up without having found out a thing!

11

"I would rather have stayed back here," he said.

"Why is that?" asked Mr Crustscrubber.

"Because . . . because of that business about the old cemetery – " Tony cleared his throat. He decided not to beat about the bush any longer, and pulled the piece of paper out of his trouser pocket.

"I would have liked to have helped with the campaign," he declared.

"You'd have liked to have helped?" said Mr Crustscrubber in surprise and obvious delight. Then, after a pause, he said, "We'll talk about that afterwards, Tony – when our little session is over."

"Afterwards?"

"You haven't come to see me to talk about the old cemetery!"

Tony pressed his lips together and fell silent. What could he say in reply to that?

And so Mr Crustscrubber continued to ask him lots of questions about the ruins and the little hotel, his father's crushed fingers and what the examination at the hospital had revealed.

Tony became more and more monosyllabic. Yes, one of the fingers had been broken. Yes, now Dad had his hand in plaster – and so on . . .

A Couple of Specimens Left...

Then at last the professional curiosity of the psychologist seemed to be satisfied. In quite a different, somehow more confidential tone of voice, he said: "So you would like to join our campaign to save the old cemetery, would you?"

"Join?" Tony hesitated. "Actually I would like to know more about it first."

"Very good!" Mr Crustscrubber said in approval. "That's just what more people ought to do: Find out about a thing and then – act!" He rubbed his hands together. "And we have acted!" he continued with pride in his voice. "Four hundred signatures we've collected and with them, we've shown that over-keen nightwatchman and his gardener just what we think about their so-called 'improvements to the cemetery'!"

"Is there a membership fee to pay to join you?" asked Tony cautiously.

"Membership fee? No!" Mr Crustscrubber rejected the suggestion. "All you need to bring with you is energy and determination!"

"Energy and determination?"

"And how!"

"But the excavation works have been stopped now – or isn't that true?" asked Tony, his heart beating.

"Yes indeed, thanks to *our* petition!" said Mr Crustscrubber. Then quietly and mysteriously he added, "But that's not the only thing our campaign is out to achieve, not by a long chalk!"

"It isn't? What else is there?"

Mr Crustscrubber glanced over to the door, as if he were afraid of being overheard. Then he said in a whisper, "Yes, I can tell you about it. It's all to do with my treatment course."

Tony went pale. "Your treatment course?"

"Yes!" Mr Crustscrubber felt in one of the drawers and pulled out a fat, black file.

"You know, don't you," he said confidentially, "that I have developed a course to combat phobia. And I *must* find out whether it works!"

Heavy with misgiving, Tony asked, "But what's that got to do with the old cemetery?"

"Oh, it's got a lot to do with it!" answered Mr Crustscrubber. "Surely you remember that I asked you whether you know any vampires?"

Tony nodded anxiously.

"Unfortunately, to my deep disappointment, you said you did not know any. But in the meantime, I have found out that there really are a couple of specimens left of this ancient species – right here in our town!"

"What!" exclaimed Tony. "Vampires – in our town?"

Mr Crustscrubber nodded.

"Have you . . . seen these vampires?" inquired Tony, his voice trembling.

Once more, Mr Crustscrubber nodded. But then he knitted his eyebrows and said, "Not *vampires* – vampire!"

Tony could hardly contain his curiosity. But he forced himself to stay calm.

"One vampire?" he asked, as casually as he could. "Where – in the old cemetery?"

"No, here at my practice!" answered Mr Crustscrubber. "He came to me as a patient!"

"A patient?" For a second, Tony was speechless.

"But one thing irritates me about the whole matter," continued Mr Crustscrubber. "He will insist that he is not a vampire at all!"

Mr Crustscrubber had got up from his revolving chair and was now striding backwards and forwards, the rubber soles of his shoes squeaking unbearably.

"Would you like to know how I succeeded in confirming that he *is* a vampire after all?"

Mr Crustscrubber showed Tony a small brown leather case. "Here, with the help of this hand mirror," he declared. "I combed my hair and while I was doing it, I looked in the mirror, and just imagine: he had *no* reflection!"

Mr Crustscrubber laughed in a self-satisfied manner and asked, "Now, what do you say to that?"

"I, er — " Tony was at a loss for words. His mind was racing feverishly: Did he know the vampire who had come here as a patient? Which vampire could it have been? Gregory? William the Wild? Frederick the Frightful? It certainly couldn't have been Rudolph, because Tony would have heard about that, even if only from Anna!

There was a knock at the door, and after an irritated, "What is it?" from the psychologist, Mrs Crustscrubber appeared in the room.

"I don't want to disturb you," she said, "but Mrs Carmichael has already been waiting for a quarter of an hour."

"Mrs Carmichael?" Mr Crustscrubber glanced at his huge wristwatch. "Oh, it's so late already!" he said guiltily. "What's more, we still had so much to talk about. Would you care to come back again, Tony?"

"Me?" Tony thought of the mystery patient. "Yes, I would!" he assured him. "But . . . could it not be too early?"

"What do you mean, not too early?"

"Well . . . I spend so much time outside with my friends nowadays in the afternoons. That's why I would rather not come until the evening." *After sunset!* he added to himself.

"Well, we'll see what we can arrange," said Mr Crustscrubber. "I will have to talk to your parents about it."

"To my parents? But it's up to me!"

"That's true," said Mr Crustscrubber. "And *you* think you still have things to discuss with me too, do you?"

"Oh yes!" replied Tony quickly. "The holiday – after all, I was very disappointed about it – and the cemetery campaign too, of course!"

16

Bottled Up Problems

Tony's mother was already waiting for him in the car.

"Well, how did it go?" she asked.

"Just as it should have gone," said Tony evenly. But all the time he was quivering inside from Mr Crustscrubber's revelations.

His mother started the car irritably. "It's really quite impossible to have a reasonable conversation with you!" she scolded.

Tony grinned. "I have been having an excellent conversation with Mr Crustscrubber."

"Have you?" She looked at him searchingly. "What about?"

Tony made an expansive gesture. "Oh, about the holiday and Dad's squashed fingers . . . and that I am very disappointed about it all . . . "

"Really?" Now her expression changed, and with obvious relief she said, "I'm so pleased, Tony, that you aren't bottling up your problems any more, and that you are giving Mr Crustscrubber the chance to work through them and discuss them."

"But he needs to give me a lot more time!"

"What . . . a lot more time?"

"Yes! We had hardly started to talk properly when the

next patient arrived. And what's more — " Tony pulled the little card that Mrs Crustscrubber had given him from his pocket. "I can go back on Friday – that's in three days' time."

"But Tony," said his mother, "first you couldn't bear the thought of going to see Mr Crustscrubber, and now it seems you can hardly wait for the next appointment!"

"Exactly!" said Tony. "Because I don't want to bottle up my problems any longer."

And especially not the problem of which vampire could be Mr Crustscrubber's patient, he added to himself.

What Tony would really have liked to do, once he was back home, was to ring up Mr Crustscrubber and ask him the name of the vampire. But he suspected that the psychologist would not be willing to give information over the telephone and would put him off till Friday's appointment.

So now Tony was even more impatient to see the Little Vampire and his sister Anna!

The Coffin Shift had taken place on Sunday night – two nights ago – and Tony knew that it had all gone well from a letter from Anna, which he had discovered by his window on Monday morning.

We've all arrived safely back in the vault, she had written. *Now we have to make an inventory again, and then we'll be able to see each other – soon!*

Your own, very happy, Anna.

Soon! Tony gave a deep sigh. If only it were this evening!

Flying Saucer

As it began to grow dark, Tony took out his book *The Vampire from Amsterdam* and lay down on his bed. He switched on the bedside light and began to read "The Horror under the Cellar Stairs". It was a story about a man who moved into an old house which had been standing empty for a long time. It was supposed to be haunted . . . Tony read how one day the man heard a rumbling noise in the cellar. He opened the cellar door and peered down into the damp, mouldy-smelling darkness when suddenly – there was a knock.

Tony gave a start. Hastily he jumped off his bed and ran to the window. But then the knock came again, louder this time, and he heard his father's voice, "Tony? Are you asleep yet?"

"Oh, it's you," growled Tony and got back into bed.

"May I come in?" asked Dad.

"If it's absolutely necessary . . . "

The bedroom door opened and Tony's father came in. "Were you expecting somebody else?" he asked in amusement, glancing at the window, where Tony still had not drawn the curtains. "A vampire perhaps?"

It was his father's usual way of making jokes about things he did not believe in, and which he thought were "figments of the imagination".

19

"A vampire?" said Tony sarcastically. "No, I was waiting for a flying saucer, so I could at least have a bit of an adventure during these holidays!"

His father looked at him, startled. Then his face took on a rather guilty expression. "Tony!" he said, sitting on the edge of the bed. "Believe me, I would have loved to hvae stayed on in the Vale of Doom, too." He shot a troubled look at his right hand, which was in plaster right up over his knuckles. "But with a broken finger . . ." He tried to laugh. "At any rate, I would find it a great pity," he went on, "if our relationship were to turn sour because of this . . . well, this somewhat unfortunate holiday."

"What?" exclaimed Tony, pretending to be scared. "You've got a problem with your relationship now – you and Mum?"

"Mum and me? No! I was talking about *our* relationship! The activity holiday in the Vale of Doom was supposed to help both of *us* grow closer to one another. And at the beginning, everything did go brilliantly – we got on very well together, I thought. Until this business with my fingers."

Tony said nothing, just twisted the corners of his mouth doubtfully.

Good News

"And as far as your tent and your sleeping-bag are concerned," Tony's father went on, "you'll be able to make good use of them again in the autumn."

"In the autumn?"

"Yes, because then we'll be going on another activity holiday!"

"Where?" asked Tony distrustfully.

"Where?" Dad smirked. "Back to the Vale of Doom, of course, and Wolf's Hollow!"

'I – I won't be able to," answered Tony hastily; for if the Little Vampire was not going to be there too in the ruins in the Vale of Doom, there was nothing whatsoever to tempt him back again!

"You won't be able to?" said his father, puzzled.

"No! In the autumn, our class are going on a trip," Tony explained. "And anyway, I don't really want to."

His father looked at him in astonishment.

"You really are a mystery to me," he said. "Just now you had a face as long as a month of wet Mondays, because we had to cut short our holiday in the Vale of Doom by a week . . . And then, when I bring you the good news that we could make up for it all in the autumn, you aren't in the least bit pleased."

"It's just that I've had quite enough of the Vale of Doom!" said Tony firmly.

"And your party?" asked Dad. "Are you fed up with that idea too?"

"What party?" Tony hesitated.

"The party you can have here at home with all your friends."

Now Tony did give a grin. "Yeah, with *all* my friends!" he said, remembering he still had not invited Anna and Rudolph. Anyhow, he was not allowed to hold the party until his father had recovered.

"Are you better already, then?" he asked cautiously.

"Oh yes, much better!" answered his father. "Since I've been wearing this plaster, it has hardly hurt at all. And that's why we're going to let you have your party next Saturday!"

"Next Saturday?"

He hoped that the Little Vampire and his family would not be holding their Coming Home party in the vault the same evening! Anna had invited him to it when they were in the Vale of Doom. Not that Tony intended going to a Coming Home party in the Sackville-Bagg family vault . . . but if the vampires were having their own celebration, Anna and Rudolph would certainly not be able to come to Tony's party, and he just couldn't imagine a party without the pair of them!

"You don't seem very excited about that either!" His father's voice sounded disappointed.

"Oh, I am!" Tony assured him. "I'm – I'm just thinking who I'm going to invite."

"Is that so difficult?" asked Dad.

"Mmm, it is rather," said Tony slowly. Then he added with a grin, "For instance, how many vampires shall I invite – one, or two . . . "

"Or three, or four," added his father, smiling. He obviously thought Tony was joking.

"I'd better not," said Tony seriously. "Or do you want me to invite Anna and Rudolph's grandfather, William the Wild, or their grandmother, Sabina the Sinister?"

"William the Wild? Sabina the Sinister?" repeated Dad, laughing louder than ever. "Well, those are some strange names! But luckily, your funny friend Rudolph and his sister Anna, with their vampire fancy-dress and their extraordinary relations have gone somewhere else! And that leaves your nicest friends!" he added cheerfully. "Ollie, Sebastian, Henry . . . What about writing out the invitations now, so that they'll be free to come next Saturday?"

"Not a bad idea," agreed Tony.

"Then I won't keep you from your work any longer!" Dad stood up and went over to the door.

"What time should the party start?" asked Tony.

"After sunset, naturally," joked his father.

"After sunset?" Tony grinned. "OK. But you can take the blame!"

Dear Anna, Dear Rudolph

"That leaves my nicest ones?" said Tony, when his father had left the room. "The nicest ones have just come back, you mean!" He sat down at his desk, took out his best writing paper – the blood-red sort – and began:

Dear Anna, dear Rudolph,
   I would be so pleased if you could both come to my party next Saturday.
Starting time: after sunset.
Yours, Tony

Then Tony wrote out four more invitations, although on plainer paper. To Ollie and Tanya, Henry and Sebastian. Then after thinking it over for a minute, he tore up Tanya's invitation because of Anna.

As Tony put the invitations into their envelopes and wrote the names on the front, he realized once more how much the vampires were at a disadvantage: he'd probably bump into Olly, Sebastian and Henry out on the street tomorrow, or at the latest on Monday, when school started again. But Tony would have to wait for Anna and Rudolph – wait, until they knocked on his window. And this evening, it seemed Anna and Rudolph had something more important arranged . . .

Sad and disappointed, Tony finally crept into bed, after he had kept himself awake for such a long time with *The Vampire from Amsterdam* and "The Horror under the Cellar Stairs" that the words seemed to be dancing in front of his eyes.

"Let's just hope they come tomorrow!" he sighed, with a last longing look at the window.

You Must Help Me!

"Hey! Stand up!" called a harsh voice, which Tony seemed to recognize. "Come on, will you stand up please!" It was the voice of . . . Mr Flyswotter, Tony's maths teacher!

"No, I don't want to add up!"

"Oh, but you *are* going to add up!" answered Mr Flyswotter, and he banged on the desk with his pointer. "Come up here to the board and add this up!"

"No, I won't!" cried Tony – and then he woke up. It was the middle of the night: moonlight was filtering through the curtains into his room, and there was not a sound to be heard from the other rooms in the flat. But wait a minute . . . suddenly someone knocked loudly and energetically against the window pane.

Tony jumped out of bed and ran to the window. He tore the curtains to one side – and found himself gazing into the pale face of the Little Vampire!

Quickly Tony opened the window.

"You took long enough!" hissed the Little Vampire. "I was beginning to think you'd gone into hibernation!"

"Hallo, Rudolph!" said Tony, puzzled at the extraordinary appearance of the Little Vampire. His hair, which usually hung down in long strands over his shoulders, had been treated with something which made it lie flat against his head and glisten greasily. What was more – Tony coughed – it smelt quite unvampirish, as if Rudolph had come straight from a hairdresser's salon!

"You must help me!" announced the Little Vampire huskily, and climbed down from the window-sill into the room.

"Help you? How?" asked Tony warily.

"*Help me? How?*" the vampire mimicked him. "Haven't you any eyes in your head?"

" 'Course I have! Why?"

"Can't you see that Wally the Wicked has ruined my hairstyle?"

"Wally did that?"

"Yes," said the Little Vampire in a cavernous voice. "At that awful Nail Competition. I wish I'd never gone along!"

"What has the Nail Competition got to do with it?"

The Little Vampire threw him a dark look. "Ha! Everyone won something – George got first prize, that was a blanket, Wally the second prize, that was a pillow, and Greg got third prize, a button from George's button collection. It was only me who came out of it with nothing, yet again! And then Wally said I ought to get a consolation prize . . . "

"A consolation prize?"

"Yes!" growled the Little Vampire. "George the Boisterous took some disgusting hair cream out from under his cloak and Wally started to 'console' me . . . "

"How?" asked Tony in surprise.

"You still can't guess? By smearing my hair with the hair cream, you dumbhead!"

"So *that's* the consolation prize?" Tony was shocked. "Booby prize, more like!"

"Yes! They're all boobies – George and Wally and their stupid Men's Club!" The Little Vampire had worked himself up into quite a rage, and he had every reason, thought Tony.

"So now I'm forced to wash my hair," the vampire continued grimly. "For the first time in thirty-eight years!"

"You want to wash your hair?" repeated Tony uneasily. "You don't mean here – at my home?"

"Where else am I going to do it?" hissed the Little Vampire. "Have you ever seen such a thing as a tap in the vault?"

"No," Tony admitted, "but my parents—"

"No problem! I'll be very quiet," replied the Little Vampire. "Come on, take me to the bathroom!"

"Well you can only do it in the basin," said Tony. "The spray on the bath makes much too much noise. And you can't use the hairdrier either!"

"Hairdrier?" said the vampire, looking at him blankly. "I said I wanted to *wash* my hair! Now come on, I've been waiting for this for four nights!"

"For four nights?"

"Yes, that's how long I've had to keep the stuff on."

"Why?"

"Why, why! Because that was part of the booby prize! And Greg made sure I kept to it! So come on, will you?" he went on in a determined voice. "Or would you rather I did it on my own?"

"N – no!" said Tony hastily. He ran to the door, opened it cautiously and listened. There was not a sound.

"All's quiet! We can go," he whispered to the vampire. They crossed the darkened passage on tiptoe. Not until they had closed the bathroom door behind them did Tony dare switch on the light.

Hmm, That Does Smell Nice...

"So where are the hairwashing things?" asked the Little Vampire impatiently.

Tony, whose eyes still had not quite got used to the sudden brightness, groped blindly for the bottle at the side of the bath. "Here!"

The Little Vampire gave a shriek. "Are you trying to kill me?"

"I – I'm sorry!" stammered Tony. Someone had put the brown bottle of suncream on the edge of the bath!

"There – the shampoo's over there!" he said in embarrassment and picked up a green bottle, with *Herbal Shampoo for Meadow-fresh Hair* written on it, from the other side of the bathtub.

The Little Vampire unscrewed the top and sniffed. "Yuk!" he said in disgust. "That pongs even worse than the hair cream!"

"We do have one other kind," replied Tony. "You use it when . . . " Out of the cupboard, he took a bottle of mud shampoo, which his mother occasionally used, " . . . you have greasy hair."

"Greasy hair?" repeated the Little Vampire and

giggled. "I have super-greasy hair! Does it help?"

"It's guaranteed to," said Tony with a grin. "Here, doesn't it stink?'

But the Little Vampire had his own ideas about what smelt revolting. He unscrewed the top and then said with a rapturous expression, "Hmmm, that smells lovely . . . sort of rotten and boggy!"

Straightaway he squeezed a large dollop of the shampoo on to his hand and rubbed it around with his fingernails.

"Hey, don't take so much!" said Tony. "Mum bought that in a health shop, and it cost the earth!"

"Stingy!" grumbled the vampire. Then he asked grumpily, "Well then, when are you going to start?"

"Me?" Tony was puzzled. "It's *you* who's going to wash your hair!"

The vampire gave a broad grin. "It's *you* who's going to wash *my* hair!"

"Me – you?" Tony gulped. "That's a good one! I'm not your servant!"

"OK, if you don't want to — " The Little Vampire moved to the bath and picked up the shower attachment. "I can wash my hair by myself . . . but only over the bath and only with this brilliant shower thing!"

Tony tried to take the shower away from him. "That makes too much noise!" he said. "My parents'll wake up!"

"Will they?" The Little Vampire clicked his pointed teeth. "But their bedroom is miles away – right the other end of the passage."

"Yes, well . . . the neighbours might hear. The one who lives below us, Mrs Grumpson, is really awful!"

"Oh? What would she do that's so awful, old Grumpbag?"

"Her husband must be over eighty and he's almost deaf. But she can hear a flea cough, or so my Dad says. And then she always sends her husband up, and he shouts and yells out on the stairway."

"She can hear a flea cough? How sweet!" said the Little Vampire. "Do you think I could pay her a visit one day?"

Tony shrugged. "No idea. But we ought to get on with it!" He hung the shower back on the hook at the end of the bath. "I'll run some water in the basin, and then I'll wash your hair."

"What are we waiting for?"

The Little Vampire sat on the edge of the bath and drummed his feet expectantly.

"Is the water nice and warm?" he asked.

"Yes!" said Tony, who was letting the water run over the back of his hands so that it didn't make a splash.

"We only have ice-cold water at home," said the vampire. "Those poor little flowers!"

Tony looked at him blankly. "What poor little flowers?"

"The ones in the cemetery! They hate cold water – just as much as we do."

"Of course, we don't like warm water much, either," the Little Vampire went on, "but on this occasion . . . what must be, must be!" He gave a deep sigh. Then he muttered, "Hey, the tap's running very slowly!"

"I haven't turned it full on," replied Tony, "because of old Grumpson."

"You are really very thoughtful!" giggled the vampire. "I wouldn't have believed it!"

Tony threw him a grim look, but didn't bother to reply.

Tony the Hairdresser

At last the basin was full of water.

"Now we can start," said Tony, gritting his teeth.

"And how am I supposed to put my head in there?" asked the Little Vampire.

"You're only supposed to dangle your hair in the water," answered Tony.

"Dangle my hair in the water?" said the vampire, helplessly. "How do I do that?"

"You stand in front of the basin, bend your head over and then your hair will hang into the water."

"Oh I see . . . " murmured the vampire. Then after a moment's consideration, he said suspiciously, "But then my neck will be totally unprotected . . . "

Tony grinned. "Don't worry, *I'm* certainly not going to do anything to you!"

"But what about the others? After all, I'm helpless if I stand with my head bent over like that!" said the Little Vampire piteously.

"What others? For a start, my parents are asleep and anyway, the bathroom door is locked."

"Hmmm," went the vampire, and he studied the basin of water very uneasily. "Is there really no other way of doing it?"

"Yes—"

"What's that?" asked the vampire hopefully.

"Well, you could use a dry shampoo. Then your hair would look as if it had been washed."

"Really?" exclaimed the Little Vampire. "And I wouldn't have to stick my head in a basin of water?"

"No. But afterwards . . . your scalp itches."

"What? It itches?" The Little Vampire gave an impatient snort. "But that's just why I came here in the first place – to get rid of this horrible itching once and for all!"

"Well," Tony pointed to the basin, "then there's nothing else for it!"

"If you think so . . . " said the vampire plaintively. He came over to the basin and bent his head so that his hair dangled in the water.

Meanwhile, Tony was unscrewing the bottle of mud shampoo. He was just about to pour out a little when the Little Vampire shot up into the air crying, "My eyes! I mustn't get any water in my eyes!"

"And definitely not any shampoo either!" Tony added under his breath, but thought he had better not say it aloud.

"Here," he said, and gave the vampire a flannel. "You must press this firmly against your eyes. Then nothing will get in."

"All right!" The vampire pressed the flannel to his eyes and bent over the basin once more.

This time, Tony could push the vampire's shoulder-length hair more deeply into the warm water. It was greasy and unbelievably tangled. Tony shuddered. The touch of that hair . . . ugh! And the smell too, a mixture of hair cream and Rudolph's normal vampire pong . . .

He took a blob of mud shampoo about the size of a

walnut and spread it all over the wet hair – without the slightest effect. It didn't even begin to lather!

"Hey, what's the matter?" groaned the Little Vampire. His voice sounded strangely muffled and distorted through the flannel.

"It's the shampoo. It won't lather."

"Then use some more – why not use the whole bottle?"

"The whole bottle!" Tony coughed indignantly. "Then I'd have to spend all my pocket money buying a new one!"

"Are you my friend or aren't you?" said the Little Vampire.

" 'Course I am." Tony took about twice as much shampoo again. This time a thin film of bubbles began to form. By now, the stink in the bathroom had become so unbearable that Tony was afraid he was going to pass out.

He clenched his teeth and squeezed and rubbed at the hair until the water in the basin looked as black as Rudolph's cloak. Then, with a sigh of relief, he pulled out the plug.

"Finished!" he announced, as the water slowly began to run away with a glug and a gurgle.

"Finished?" The Little Vampire raised his head. He fingered his hair suspiciously. Now it had been washed, it was even more matted than before, but that only seemed to please him.

"That's great! It's so tangly!" he said enthusiastically. "And it doesn't itch any more – not even a little bit!"

He looked at Tony and a happy smile spread over his face.

"Tony Peasbody, you're an expert hairdresser!"

Get Some Practice In First

Then straight away, as if he found it painful to have said something nice, he said to Tony, "Now, you must give me a neck massage!"

He bent over the basin once more. "Come on, get on with it!" he hissed. "My neck is as stiff as a coffin's board!"

"Massage your neck?" Tony gave a dry laugh. "You must think you're the Honourable Percy Pigsbubble, and I'm the ghost of your servant!"

"Me? The Honourable Percy?" The Little Vampire straightened himself and gazed at Tony. "That's the nicest thing you've ever said to me, Tony!" he said with a sigh of great emotion. "Me – a Pigsbubble! Oh, I wish Olga had heard that!"

"You'd do better to get your hair dry!" growled Tony, handing the vampire a large bath-towel – one of his own, so there wouldn't be any trouble.

The Little Vampire took the towel and sniffed it. "Phew!" he said contemptuously. "This smells revolting! What on earth does your mum do your washing with?"

"That I don't know," said Tony with a grin. "Because in this house, it's my dad who does the washing, not Mum!"

The Little Vampire threw him a furious look. "What am I supposed to do with this stinky cloth?" he said, whirling the towel around Tony's head.

Tony grinned even more. "What indeed! Rub your hair dry, of course! And your cloak, as well!" he added, for the vampire's cloak had got rather wet.

"What, my cloak?" Rudolph looked down at himself in shock. "Oh, bother!" he said. "If it gets any wetter, I'll have to go on foot!"

He began to rub his cloak energetically – instead of first drying his hair, which would have been far more sensible. Then suddenly he stopped.

"What am I bothering to do this for?" he said, giving a pleased smile. "I've got another cloak with me as well!" With that, he felt under his cloak and pulled out a second, dry one.

"Actually, I brought it for you," he said. "But now I'll have to think of myself first – of course."

He slipped off his own, dripping wet cloak, laid it over the edge of the bath, and pulled on the second one. "The other is for you!" he said graciously.

"For me?" said Tony indignantly. "I suppose you want me to crash!"

"No." The Little Vampire clicked his teeth together contentedly. "I want you to get it dry. I'm sure when you're older, you'll be doing the washing, just like your father. So get some practice in first . . ."

Tony gave a furious snort. "Huh! At least I won't be such a male chauvinist pig as you!" he said angrily.

"Won't you?" said the vampire, unusually gently. "I don't know exactly what a male chauvinist pig is, but I reckon — " He got no further, for at that moment a door banged at the end of the passage.

"My parents!" stammered Tony.

The Little Vampire drew in his breath and his eyes darted round the bathroom. Then he tore open the window and, without another word, spread out his arms and flew away.

Making Allowances

"Tony?" It was Mum's voice. "Aren't you well?"

Tony quickly shut the window.

"No," he answered. Indeed he did feel very wretched. The bathroom looked horrific . . . It would take at least half an hour to mop up the floor and clean out the basin. And what was more, Tony had used up almost all the mud shampoo. He hastily put the shampoo bottle back in the cupboard. There was no need for his mother to find out straight away about the shampoo, at least!

"What are you doing in there?" she asked, now sounding more impatient. "Why aren't you in bed?"

"I needed the bathroom!" replied Tony. It wasn't very original, but it was true enough.

"Is something wrong?"

You could say that! thought Tony. Out loud, he said, "No, nothing too bad."

"Nothing too bad?" she repeated, and instead of knocking as she usually did, she pushed at the door handle.

"You've locked the door!" she exclaimed.

Tony did not answer. He quickly picked up the flannel and the towel, which the vampire had dropped carelessly on the floor, and hung them over the towel rail. Now he had to get rid of the vampire cloak. After a moment's thought, he stuffed it in the red plastic bucket under the basin.

"Tony! Why have you locked the door?" His mother's voice sounded agitated.

"Why? Because I've now reached the age when you do lock the door!" he answered. "And what's more, I hate it when people snoop around me!"

"This has got nothing to do with snooping. I'm worried about you, and simply want to know if everything is all right!" retorted his mother. "It's especially not snooping when you lock yourself in the bathroom at half past two in the morning," she added.

She paused, before saying vigorously, "Now, will you please open this door!"

The whole time Tony had been wondering how he was going to explain to his mother why the tiles were dripping, the towel was soaking wet and the basin caked with dirt! At last he had an idea. He gave the tap a quick turn and held his hair under the warm stream of water. Then he wrapped the wet towel round his head and opened the bathroom door.

His mother plunged inside – she seemed to be quite angry! "Can this be true?" she cried. "Washing your hair in the middle of — " But she never finished the sentence. She just gazed round the bathroom in disbelief.

Tony had retreated to the edge of the bath. His parents were against smacking children, it was true – but every now and then it happened that they "lost control of their hands" as they put it. And at this moment, Tony's mother looked so annoyed that she might well "lose control" . . .

"This is the end!" she exclaimed, and her voice shook with indignation. "You start washing your hair in the middle of the night, you leave the bathroom awash and

44

then — " She broke off and sniffed the air testily, "on top of it all, you use my mud shampoo! Just tell me this, are you completely out of your mind?"

"No, but I nearly was," replied Tony.

His mother looked at him irritably. "You nearly were? What's that supposed to mean?"

"I was having a nightmare," Tony explained. "I was dreaming that my whole head was full of – er – lice, and the lice were biting me and . . . sucking my blood. And there were more and more lice coming – and suddenly, I woke up right here, next to the basin. Yes, and my hair was all wet, and the floor was sopping . . . "

"You came into the bathroom without realizing it – like a sleepwalker?"

Tony nodded.

"But you've never sleepwalked before!" said his mother, half shocked, half in disbelief. "Why on earth should you suddenly start to do so tonight?"

"Well, 'cos the dream was so frightening," Tony replied. "All those lice . . . they really did drive me out of bed and I must have just washed my hair in my sleep!"

"Lice . . . sucking your blood," said his mother, shaking her head. "And all because you will read those frightful vampire stories! I bet it was the book Mrs Goody gave you, *The Vampire from* . . . – I can't remember where – that gave you the nightmare!"

Tony did not contradict her – it seemed wisest not to. It was very strange: If he had told her the truth – in other words that the wet and dirt in the bathroom weren't his fault – his mother would not have believed him. And yet she appeared to believe his excuse that he had had a nightmare and sleepwalked. And even if she was not completely convinced by the story of the bad dream, at least she had made allowances for him!

45

Telephone

"I'll clear it all up in the morning," Tony offered.

"In the morning? Oh no, this has to be done here and now!" retorted his mother.

"Here and now?" said Tony.

"You're not thinking of getting out of clearing it up, I hope?"

"No. It's just that I'm dead tired."

"I see, and I'm supposed to clear it all up by myself, am I?" asked Mum frostily.

"No," said Tony with a grin. "You could wake Dad up!"

"I should think he's been woken up ages ago," Mum snapped. "With all the noise you've been making down here, no one could get any sleep!"

And as if to confirm her words, at that moment the telephone began to ring.

Tony's mother paled. "Who can that be?" she murmured. Then she said, full of misgiving, "Oh yes, I can just imagine who . . . " She hurried out of the bathroom and Tony heard her running across the passage to the living-room. The phone was still ringing.

As soon as the ringing had stopped, Tony took the wet vampire cloak out of the bucket and crept on tiptoe to his bedroom. There he emptied his sportsbag, stuffed the cloak inside it and put the bag in his cupboard. Then just as quietly, he ran back to the bathroom. At the door, he waited for a minute and listened.

"Yes, of course Mrs Grumpson," he heard his mother saying. "Please, I do apologize. It will never happen again. Certainly not, Mrs Grumpson."

"*No, certainly not Mrs Grumpson!*" said Tony in his mother's tone of voice. He picked up the red plastic bucket, plonked it in the bath with a loud bang and turned on the taps. And just as Tony had expected, his mother came rushing into the bathroom and turned them off.

"For heaven's sake, Tony, go and get into bed at once!" she snapped.

"Into bed?" He pretended to be surprised. "You just said we had to clear up all the mess. That's why — " he pointed to the bucket with a grin, "— I was running the water."

"We'll have to put it off till tomorrow morning," replied his mother. "Or do you want Mrs Grumpson to call the police?"

"The police?" said Tony in pretend fright.

"Yes! She threatened to call the police if we went on making so much noise."

Tony grinned to himself contentedly. What he had not managed to do, Mrs Grumpson had. And tomorrow morning he would sleep late: after all, it was a holiday!

"All right then. *Good* night!" he said.

He wound a dry towel round his wet hair, and happily marched back to his bedroom.

Too Demanding

As it happened, the next day began in the most tiresome way for Tony, with the persistent, discordant bleeping of his alarm clock. Tony woke with a start, feeling very cross. His mother must have secretly set his alarm for him!

Angrily, he pushed down the alarm button. One look at the clock face showed him that it was still far too early to get up: half past eight – it was a terrible cheek to wake him up at this time during the holidays!

Then Tony noticed that there was a note beside his bed. He began to read suspiciously:

Dear Tony,

Dad and I have gone to town to do some shopping. You had better get up straight away, because you've got a lot to do.

Scrub the basin and wipe down the tiles. When you've finished, you can go and buy some bread rolls. There's money on the kitchen table. Bye for now – and we expect the bathroom to be shipshape when we come home!

Mum and Dad

"Shipshape indeed!" grumbled Tony. When a day

started as badly as this, it was best to stay in bed! He swallowed carefully a couple of times . . . perhaps he had a sore throat?

But his throat didn't hurt at all.

No, he was feeling so wretched this morning "for emotional reasons", as Mr Crustscrubber would say. So far, everything had gone wrong. Because of the hairwashing, he had never asked Rudolph about Mr Crustscrubber's vampire patient whose identity was shrouded in mystery. Nor had he given Rudolph the invitation to his party. And now, to top it all, he had to clean up the bathroom all by himself . . . Tony sighed and got out of bed.

He dressed and went to the bathroom. Secretly he hoped that his parents had cleared it up after all. But the bathroom looked just as mucky as it had during the night. They hadn't even swilled out the basin! Had they washed and cleaned their teeth in the kitchen then? But Tony couldn't have cared less. He fetched his radio from his bedroom and set to work.

He only gave it a superficial clean-up. His parents would simply see that this job was – to use another of Mr Crustscrubber's favourite phrases – "just too demanding" for him.

Afterwards, Tony took the money to get the rolls and left the flat, feeling that the day could now only get better. Unfortunately, he was wrong.

In the afternoon, his mother decided that he must come with her to apologize to Mrs Grumpson and take her a huge bunch of flowers. Tony had to sit on Mrs Grumpson's hard sofa next to his mother for a whole hour, drinking hot chocolate that was much too sweet and eating cakes that tasted as if they'd gone off. And that still wasn't the end of it. That evening, when Tony wanted to watch the film *The Wolf That Was Really a Man* for a well-deserved rest, his mother said indignantly, "A werewolf film? No, that's quite out of the question – after that terrible nightmare you had last night!"

"But I dreamed about *lice*," Tony objected – but in vain: Mum was not going to change her mind.

Since Tony's own television had broken down a few weeks earlier, there was nothing else for him to do but go to bed and read.

He opened *The Vampire from Amsterdam*, but after only one page, his eyes were almost shut. Tony put the book to one side and turned out the light.

Sackcloth and Ashes

All at once there was a knock.

"No, no more hair washing!" groaned Tony, still half asleep. The knocking came again, and now Tony was wide awake. He ran to the window and quickly pulled the curtains to one side.

Outside, on the window-sill, sat Anna!

Feeling a little shy, Tony opened the window.

"Hallo Tony!" said Anna.

"Hallo Anna," he answered gruffly.

She climbed nimbly into the room. "At last we can see each other again!" she said, smiling tenderly at him.

At last? thought Tony. It wasn't even a week since they had last met in the Vale of Doom! That was the evening Anna had shown him the cupboard full of old clothes in the cellars of the ruins.

And "see" was a bit of an exaggeration too, the room was so dark! Tony crossed over to his bed and switched on the bedside lamp.

"I expect you've come to collect your dress," he said. Anna did not reply. She was gazing around the room with a curiously shy look.

"It's strange," she said gently, "it all looks quite different . . ."

51

"Different?" Tony followed her look, but of course he could not see anything out of the ordinary. "What's different about it?"

"I don't know . . . Perhaps I just feel it because – I haven't been here for so long. And because it was so horrible and uncomfortable in the ruins. Oh Tony, I really am happy!" she sighed.

Tony blushed. He quickly went over to the cupboard and brought out the old white lace dress and the veil. The Little Vampire had brought them to him on the last evening of his holiday in the hotel in Happy Valley, so that he could look after them for Anna.

"Here!"

"I still can't take them," replied Anna, and a shadow flitted across her face. "You know, it's Aunt Dorothy . . . she can't stand that dress. It's unsuitable and inappropriate, that was what she said. And then she noticed that it had gone from the cupboard in the ruins. Now she's threatened to rip it into a thousand pieces if she can lay her hands on it!"

"She wants to tear it up?" asked Tony, shocked.

"Yes, but I'm not going to be put off by that," said Anna firmly. "During the Family Council this evening, I put forward a suggestion: that we vampire children shouldn't always have to go around in sackcloth and ashes. We want to be allowed to wear pretty things as well, just like Aunt Dorothy!"

"I hope your suggestion was accepted," said Tony, thinking that he would otherwise have to keep the old dress and the veil hidden in his cupboard for ever! Soon he wouldn't have any room left for his own things! He suddenly remembered Rudolph's wet cloak.

"Surely you could take this away with you," he said. He pulled his sportsbag out of the cupboard, and had to cough: Even through the bag, the stink of the wet vampire cloak was quite indescribable.

"Rudolph wanted *me* to get it dry," he explained. "But I can hardly hang it out on the line! And it's never going to dry in my cupboard."

"All right, I'll take it back to Rudolph," Anna volunteered. "And in return, you can look after my dress and my veil for a bit longer!"

The Old Vault and Some New Clubs

"The main thing is, Aunt Dorothy mustn't look for those things at my house!" worried Tony.

"Why should she?" Anna reassured him. "You know she has no idea that we two are — " She didn't say any more, just gave a low giggle.

"But Aunt Dorothy *does* know that Rudolph knows me!" Tony replied. "She was always spying on Rudolph till in the end he was banished from the vault because of it!"

"But she still doesn't know where you *live*!" said Anna vigorously. "What's more, I'll probably be able to pick up the dress and veil on Sunday."

"This Sunday?" asked Tony, pleasantly surprised.

"Yes!" Now she was smiling. "And that's also the reason I'm here now, although I really ought to be at the Family Council."

She paused, before announcing solemnly: "I would like to invite you to our Coming Home party on Sunday evening in the dear old Sackville-Bagg Family Vault!"

Tony gulped. Anna had talked about the Coming Home party back in the Vale of Doom, and about her idea of going to it with Tony as her partner: she in the lace dress, and Tony wearing the old suit that he had brought back with him from the ruins to please Anna. But Tony had told her that he was not very keen to meet all Anna's relations – and especially not in the vault!

"What about Aunt Dorothy?" he began cautiously, hoping to dissuade Anna from her plan. "Aren't you afraid she'll rip the dress to pieces as she threatened she would?"

"No!" said Anna confidently, shaking her thick, shoulder-length hair. "Firstly, the Family Council will take votes on my suggestion tonight. And I'm pretty certain the suggestion will be accepted and then at last we vampire children will be allowed to wear what *we* want! And secondly, it's a party without any grown-ups," she added. "Just you and me and Rudolph – and Greg, if he feels like it."

"Greg as well?" said Tony in dismay. "Do you think he'll want to come?"

"I've no idea," Anna replied. "You never know with Greg. You know how he is!"

Tony nodded anxiously.

"Don't you think he'll be at his Men's Club on Sunday?" he asked.

"The Men's Club is off!" replied Anna.

"Off?"

"Yes. I'm not quite sure why – only that it was something to do with the Nail Competition. Now Greg says he wants to set up a new one with Rudolph."

"A new Nail Competition?"

"No – a new Men's Club – worst luck." Anna sighed. "They'll probably be asking you soon if you'd like to join."

"Me?" said Tony, dazed. "But I hardly ever have any free time – not at night, anyway."

"They'll be asking you in any case. Mainly because then they can ask for a membership contribution."

"A membership contribution?" Tony felt his skin prickle with goosepimples. He could just guess what kind of "membership contribution" they would expect of him, as a human . . .

"I certainly won't be joining!" he declared in a croaky voice.

Anna smiled. "*We* could form a club, you know – you and I," she said. "A Romeo-and-Juliet Club!"

Tony blushed. He turned away and pretended to be looking for something on his desk.

More Questions

"But right now, I must fly," he heard Anna say.

"Already?" Tony turned around, startled.

"Yes. So see you on Sunday!" She smiled once more and spread out her arms under her cloak.

"W-wait!" said Tony quickly. "The Coming Home party you're having in the vault . . . I – I'd rather not come, if you don't mind."

Anna let her arms drop to her side.

"You'd rather not come?" she repeated. For a moment she was speechless. But then her face began to flush angrily and she exclaimed, "That's all very well for you! I've been working so hard to persuade my parents and my grandparents and my aunt to let us vampire children have a Coming Home party on our own, without grown-ups. And all for your sake, because you said you didn't want to come to a party with all my family! And now that I've managed to persuade them, you say you'd rather not come!"

Anna was so angry she screwed her hands into fists.

"I . . . " Tony wished the earth would swallow him up. "I would like to come," he said hesitantly.

"But?" prompted Anna.

"It's because of Greg," Tony confessed.

"Greg?"

Tony nodded. "In the Vale of Doom, Greg demanded that I show him how to play skittles. Then while he was playing, he broke one of his finger nails, and it was just before the Nail Competition." Tony's knees still shook as he remembered the terrifying howl Greg had given! "And then he roared that he would make me pay for it. He didn't know how, but he would think of something; something that I would never forget for the rest of my life!"

"It wasn't very nice of Greg to frighten you like that," said Anna sympathetically. Her fury with Tony seemed – thank goodness – to have blown over.

"But don't worry," she continued. "I'll sort Greg out for you!"

"Do you think that'll do any good?"

"'Course it will. Greg gets angry quickly, but he calms down just as quickly too. You shouldn't take his angry outbursts and his threats so seriously."

Not take them seriously? thought Tony doubtfully. "How are you going to . . . sort him out?" he asked.

"I'll just talk to him!" answered Anna. "If you get him at the right moment, he can be really sweet and nice."

"Really?" Tony was not convinced.

"Yes. OK then, that's sorted that one out. I'll see you Sunday, Tony!" said Anna, preparing to fly off.

"Wait, I've got one more thing to ask you," said Tony quickly. It had just occurred to him that he had wanted to ask Anna whether *she* knew anything about the mysterious vampire.

"Ask me? What about?" said Anna, looking at the window restlessly.

Tony cleared his throat. "Mr Crustscrubber, the psychologist, whom my parents go to," he began, "and I do too, sometimes," he added, just to be truthful, "Mr Crustscrubber claims he has a vampire as a patient!"

"What do you mean, 'claims'?" asked Anna impatiently. "Is it a vampire or isn't it?"

"If only I knew . . . " answered Tony. "But up till now, I haven't seen him. It seems he hasn't got a reflection!"

As he said this, he felt a slight feeling of anxiety that he had mentioned the business of not having a reflection to Anna, who went to so much trouble *not* to turn into a real vampire!

"Hasn't got a reflection?" repeated Anna.

Tony saw with relief that she did not seem to be hurt, just surprised.

"Yes, and I wanted to ask you, whether perhaps *you* know who this vampire could be?"

"Me? No! It can't be any of the family," replied Anna decisively. She picked up Rudolph's wet cloak and climbed on to the window-sill.

"But now I really must fly," she said. "Otherwise I'll be shut out of the Family Council."

She lifted her right arm, as the left one was holding Rudolph's cloak close to her. She began to move her right arm evenly up and down, till she slowly and a little bit crookedly began to rise into the air.

"See you Sunday, Tony!" she said. "By the way, I don't believe Mr Brushplugger's patient is a real vampire!" And then she was gone.

No Girls?

"Well, Tony, how about the party?" asked Tony's dad the next morning at breakfast.

Tony, who was sitting at the table in his pyjamas and sleepily stirring his cup of cocoa, pricked up his ears. "The party?" Could Dad have found out something about the vampires' Coming Home party?

His mother laughed. "You're still not properly awake! Have you forgotten that you wanted to have a party with your friends next Saturday?"

"Oh, *that* party," said Tony. "No, I haven't forgotten about it."

But there was one thing Tony had forgotten: he had forgotten to give Anna the invitation for herself and Rudolph!

"Have you given out all the invitations yet?" Dad wanted to know.

Tony gave such a violent start that he nearly knocked over his cup. "No!"

His parents exchanged looks.

"Tony probably hasn't dared ring Tanya's doorbell yet," Mum remarked, laughing as though she had made a joke.

"Wrong!" growled Tony. "I am definitely not inviting Tanya!"

"What, aren't you having any girls?" asked Mum indignantly.

"I didn't say *that*!" Tony retorted.

"Well, if it's not Tanya, which girl is it?" asked Dad curiously.

"Well — " Tony grinned. "Unfortunately I can't let you in on that just yet."

"And in any case," he continued mysteriously, "I may even invite *several* girls!"

"Several?" repeated Mum, sounding pleased. "That sounds as if you're gradually changing your attitude to girls!"

Tony looked very smug. "Firstly, you haven't the first idea what my attitude to girls is," he retorted, "and secondly, it all depends on the girl."

"Aha, so there is just *one* girl coming to the party!" Dad had picked up that clue and Tony's look gave him credit for it.

"In any case, it'll be a surprise guest," Tony answered. "In fact, there'll be two surprise guests!"

"I think you've been watching too much television," said Mum.

Tony grinned.

"But I would like to know as soon as possible who you've invited," Mum continued. "After all, the party is happening here in our flat, and so I do have a say in the matter as well!"

"Doesn't Dad?"

His father laughed. "I'm sure you'll pick out the right guests to invite."

"Picking them out is a lot easier than inviting them," said Tony and enjoyed the bewilderment on his parents' faces.

With the Very Best Intentions

And then it was Friday.

Tony woke up feeling excited, for this time he was determined to find out something about the patient whom Mr Crustscrubber claimed did not have a reflection. While he was still wondering whether or not to start talking about the campaign to "Save the Old Cemetery" and about the puzzling patient straight away, there came a knock at the bedroom door.

"Yes?" he called.

Tony's father opened the door. "Are you awake yet?" he asked.

Tony drew the bedclothes up to his chin. "No."

"Pity," murmured Dad. "I had something exciting to tell you."

"What is it?" asked Tony.

"Well," Dad came into the room and sat down on the stool by Tony's desk. "I know you're going to leap out of bed with enthusiasm at this," he began good-naturedly. "We have just decided to spend the day by the sea. After all, it is the last day of the holidays."

But as Tony continued to lie in bed, making a rather

uninspired face, Dad asked in surprise, "Why, don't you feel like it?"

Tony hesitated. It wasn't a bad suggestion; there was just one snag. "What time will we be coming back?"

"In the evening, we'll go and eat out somewhere dead trendy," suggested Dad.

"*Dead* trendy?" repeated Tony, grinning slyly. "We'll try some bad seafood, will we?"

"No," said Dad, adding reproachfully, "Honestly Tony, you know how to spoil everything, don't you!"

Tony fell silent. Should he admit that under no circumstances did he want to miss the appointment with Mr Crustscrubber? But that would raise his parents' suspicions . . . "You know how to spoil everything for *me* too!" he declared.

"What do you mean?"

"Well, you never think I might have made plans of my own. In fact, I had organized something for today."

"Well?"

"Yes. I'd fixed up to play hockey with Ollie! And then afterwards I'm going to see Mr Crustscrubber."

Tony hoped that this story would make his parents think it was the hockey with Ollie that he was keen to go to.

"Well, we could go by ourselves, Mum and I . . . " said his father. "But I didn't think you were playing hockey any more?" he added.

"Well, I want to start again!" replied Tony.

"Hmm," said Dad thoughtfully. "Mum has already rung Mr Crustscrubber and postponed the appointment to next Friday."

"What? She's rung him up?" Tony was beside himself. "Without asking me?"

Dad looked rather embarrassed.

64

"Well, you were still fast asleep," he said, not very convincingly, "and anyway, we thought you'd be pleased."

"Huh, I'm certainly *not* pleased!" growled Tony. "Not in the slightest bit."

"Tony! Stop getting so worked up!" His father tried to calm him. "It was all done with the very best intentions!"

"With the very best intentions?" repeated Tony with an indignant snort.

"Yes! You see, we remembered that you can't bear the psychologist. And that's why we said to each other we didn't want to spoil the last day of the holidays for you."

Tony drew in a deep breath. "Well that's just what you've succeeded in doing!" he cried and suddenly there were tears in his eyes. He quickly pulled up the bedclothes over his head. He heard his father get up and leave the room. Shortly afterwards, other footsteps came nearer.

A Bit of a Mystery

"Tony?" It was his mother's voice.

"What is it?" he said from under the bedclothes.

"Dad says you don't want to come to the sea with us. Is that true?"

"Yes."

"What if we ask Ollie if he'd like to come too?"

"No. I want to stay here and play hockey."

"All right then," said Mum after a pause, "if playing hockey with Ollie is more important to you . . . " She sounded very annoyed. "But then you'll have to go to Mr Crustscrubber as well!" she declared.

Tony almost gave a shriek of delight from under the bedclothes! Luckily his mother could not see how little this "threat" bothered him!

"I'll ring him back straight away and see if the appointment is still free," she announced.

Tony kicked off the bedclothes.

"I could go along later. Ollie and I wanted to play hockey for quite a long time – at least until dark."

"This interest in hockey is all rather sudden," remarked his mother.

"It was just vegetating," said Tony. "Just like you two."

"What do you mean?"

"Well, you don't do Keep Fit any more, and Dad said you've each put on two kilos since!"

His mother blushed. "We are not vegetating," she declared with dignity. "But we have so much to do at the moment and we can't just go off and do what we like – like you can!"

'Well, if that's the case," said Tony with a broad grin, "you should certainly spend the day at the sea – to have some fun, and to lose a bit of weight!"

His mother threw him a furious look.

"I'm going to make a phone call." And with these words, she bustled out of the room.

When she had gone, Tony ran over to the cupboard. From beneath Anna's lace dress, he pulled out the old hockey stick which he had not used for ages, and put it next to his desk – just in case his mother should ask about it. Then he waited impatiently for her to come back.

At last he heard her footsteps, and she came into his room.

"I've just been talking to Ollie's mother," she announced icily, and gave him one of her penetrating looks.

"Ollie's mother?" Tony was startled. Then she must have found out that he hadn't made any plans with Ollie after all . . .

"What did she say?" he asked anxiously.

"She didn't know anything at all about your arrangement! And even Ollie could only vaguely remember."

"Vaguely?" repeated Tony. Then perhaps Ollie hadn't given him away?

"At any rate, this hockey game of yours remains a bit

of a mystery!" said Mum unhappily. "But Ollie's mother said you could go over in any case, whether you'd arranged anything or not," she went on after a pause. "And she'll even drive you over to Mr Crustscrubber."

"She'll take me there?" said Tony, and his heart gave a leap of delight. His parents had obviously decided to go on their expedition without him.

"When is the appointment with Mr Crustscrubber?" he asked excitedly.

"Half-past eight," Mum replied.

Tony gasped. "As late as that?"

"Yes, the earlier appointment wasn't free any more," she explained. "And Mr Crustscrubber made an exception for you by giving you such a late appointment – only because I asked him particularly. It's the time he usually reserves for people who are working. But after all, this is the last day of your holidays, and our trip was a bit of a . . . well, a flop." Tony bit his lip, so that his mother would not see how pleased he was by this extremely fortunate arrangement.

"So we'll pick you up at quarter past nine," she finished.

Cinnamon and Sugar

An hour later Tony was standing at the edge of the street, watching his parents getting into the car. They were dressed as if they were setting off on an expedition to the North Pole: they had hiking boots, anoraks, scarves, woolly hats and gloves. It was only Dad's hand, in plaster and a sling, which looked out of place. Tony had broken out in a sweat at the sight of the thick anoraks, and he thanked his lucky stars that he was allowed to stay behind.

His mother wound down the passenger window. "Off you go to Ollie's straight away!" she said. It was a completely pointless instruction; where else was Tony going to go, since the Little Vampire would be fast asleep at this time of day!

"Yes," he mumbled.

"Have fun!" she called – and then she drove off.

"I hope so!" thought Tony with a sigh.

Ollie's mother was really very nice, thought Tony. For lunch she gave them rice pudding with cinnamon and sugar, and during the afternoon, they had cream doughnuts with chocolate sprinkled on top. They tasted particularly scrummy to Tony. His parents had recently become great enthusiasts for anything "healthy" and were constantly going on at him about sugar and white flour being bad for you. Then finally, Tony and Ollie went off to the park . . . to play football!

After tea, which wasn't bad either – they each had an enormous helping of vanilla ice-cream with hot raspberry sauce – Ollie's mum fetched her car from the garage and Tony and Ollie got in the back. Ollie's mum looked at the map.

"This Mr Crustscrubber . . . his practice is almost on the other side of town," she said.

Tony nodded. "Mum's constantly getting lost." That was not exactly true, but perhaps Ollie's mum would be influenced by it. And Tony wanted to arrive as late as possible at Mr Crustscrubber's; for if this patient who was shrouded in mystery really was a vampire, he would only be able to go to the practice *after* sunset!

But Ollie's mum did not go wrong. Much more quickly than Tony had expected – and still in the last rays of the setting sun – she drew up in front of Mr Crustscrubber's house.

Tony thanked her, and quickly, before Ollie or his mum had the idea of coming with him, he got out of the car and ran over to the door.

Puzzling Hints

It was dark in the hallway. Tony felt for the light switch and breathed a sigh of relief when he found it and the light went on. Then he rang the doorbell. Mrs Crustscrubber opened the door.

"You're here already?" she said – but unlike on his Tuesday visit, she did not ask him in.

"A friend's mother brought me over," explained Tony. The thought occurred to him that this time the hall did not smell of cauliflower. Instead there was a heavy, sweet perfume. It was a smell that so far Tony had not noticed around either Mrs Crustscrubber or her husband. There must be someone else in the practice then – someone who used this heavy scent! Perhaps it was the mysterious patient who apparently had no reflection? If it was him, then he certainly *couldn't* be a real vampire, for the sun had not yet gone down.

Tony peered past Mrs Crustscrubber at the coat hooks, in the hope of catching sight of a hat or a coat – anything, in fact, that would tell him something about the user of the perfume.

But the hooks were empty.

"Is someone still with Mr Crustscrubber?" he asked.

"There certainly is!" replied Mrs Crustscrubber,

glancing back into the hall – an anxious, fearful glance it seemed to Tony. "A rather peculiar patient," she said softly, adding, "You know, a psychologist has very many – how shall I say – extraordinary patients. And that one, who's just started coming — " She broke off and cleared her throat.

"What about him?" prompted Tony in excitement. Mrs Crustscrubber's hesitation, her anxious, frightened look, the unusual smell and now her puzzling hints had only increased his curiosity!

But Mrs Crustscrubber simply replied evasively, "It would be better if you waited outside, at the front of the house."

Outside at the front of the house? There was no way Tony was going to let himself be pushed aside!

"I – I need to go to the toilet," he said, hopping from one foot to the other as if he could hardly wait.

"You need the toilet?" repeated Mrs Crustscrubber. After a slight hesitation, she said, "Oh all right then, come in."

With a contented grin, Tony stepped into the passage.

"It's the second to last door on the left," Mrs Crustscrubber explained.

"I know," said Tony.

Face to Face

As he went along the passage, the sweetish smell grew stronger and stronger. Eeugh! It smelt as though someone had spilt a whole bottle of ancient lily-of-the-valley scent. Mr Crustscrubber's consulting room lay at the end of the passage, and it had an especially heavy padded door. Tony felt how tempting it would be to go to the door of the consulting room, open it and see who this mysterious patient really was!

But he didn't. Instead he stayed standing by the door of the toilet. It was odd: mixed in with this heavy sweet scent was the smell of dampness and decay – that particular characteristic smell that only belonged to vampires!

"Don't hang around in the passageway!" called Mrs Crustscrubber imploringly. "Go into the cloakroom! The patient might come out at any moment!"

"Excuse me?" said Tony.

"You mustn't stay out in the passage!" called Mrs Crustscrubber once more, and this time her voice sounded so urgent that Tony was afraid she might come right over to take him into the toilet herself!

"I'm just going," he said and, in slow motion, pressed the door handle downwards.

At the same time, he kept his gaze fixed on the door of the consulting room, in the hope that it would open and the patient step outside.

But nothing of the kind happened, and so there was nothing for it but to go into the small cloakroom with its green tiles. But Tony did leave the door open a chink. Then he ran to the toilet, pulled the handle and came back to his listening post next to the basin. He did not have to be patient for long.

For while the toilet was still flushing, he heard Mr Crustscrubber, and another deep, strangely rasping voice in reply.

Tony couldn't actually understand what they were talking about. But he knew that the moment had come – the moment he had been waiting for so impatiently, ever since he had first heard of the patient who supposedly had no reflection.

He was about to see him – and not through a chink in the door, either! Tony had decided to come out of the toilet as soon as the patient was in the passageway. Even so, now that the moment had almost arrived, his knees were knocking together . . . He gathered all his courage and, with his heart beating wildly, he stepped out into the passage.

"So, we'll meet again on — " he heard Mr Crustscrubber saying, but the psychologist stopped in mid-sentence.

"Tony!" he said, as surprised as if Tony had been a ghost.

"I – er, I was in the toilet," explained Tony, studying the patient standing next to Mr Crustscrubber: he was only of medium height, and dressed with old-fashioned elegance. An almost unbearably strong whiff of sweet perfume came from the man, but it was mixed with the typical smell of a vampire! Tony thought his heart would burst. There was almost no possible doubt left: he was standing opposite a vampire, a real, true vampire!

Even the stranger's looks bore it out: under a pinkish layer of powder, his face was deathly pale, and his grey, slightly red-rimmed eyes lay in deep hollows. His hair was thick and black, unnaturally black as though it had been dyed. It did not belong to his face at all, which looked old in spite of the powder – a hundred years old! thought Tony, and suddenly an icy shudder ran through him. Quickly he turned his eyes away.

"I'll go into the waiting room," he said, and without once turning round, he hurried up the passage. Only after he had closed the waiting room door behind him did his heartbeat grow steadier, and he was able to think clearly again. A vampire, a real vampire in Mr Crustscrubber's practice . . . But how could this vampire leave his coffin before the sun had set?

Laid On a Bit Thick

Tony was in the middle of all these thoughts when the door opened. He sprang up from the chair in fright, but it was only Mrs Crustscrubber.

"You can go into the consulting room now," she said.

Tony followed her slowly, worried that the vampire might still be in the building. Their brief meeting had been enough to make Tony feel a violent dislike, even fear, towards him, and he had not the slightest desire to see him again! But, to his relief, the passage was empty. Only the tell-tale smell of decay, mixed with the sweet, heavy perfume, still hung in the air.

In the consulting room, where Mr Crustscrubber was sitting behind his large, untidy desk, this smell was so strong that it made Tony cough.

"Take a seat!" said Mr Crustscrubber, his eyes twinkling at Tony in a friendly way.

Tony sat down. With a beating heart, he noticed that the fat folder – the one containing the course of treatment against phobias – lay on the desk in front of Mr Crustscrubber.

"Well, Tony?" said Mr Crustscrubber.

He was obviously expecting Tony to start without any prompting. Tony hesitated. On one hand, he was bursting to start talking about the weird patient. On the other, he only had the appointment with Mr Crustscrubber because he wanted to tell him about the problems he was pretending to have, stemming from the holiday.

"I – it's about my holiday," he began.

"Yes?"

"Well, it doesn't make me so cross any more."

"Oh, really?"

"No. I've been thinking about the holiday, and I've decided it was fun after all. And Dad couldn't help it that his hand got squashed."

Secretly, Tony gave a deep sigh. It was considerably more difficult to talk about problems that you didn't have than to talk about the ones that really did exist!

"I see," said Mr Crustscrubber.

"And the fact that you couldn't use your tent," he asked after a pause. "Aren't you disappointed about that?"

With some difficulty, Tony stifled a grin. "Well, I am a bit, of course," he said, "but not *that* much. I think my parents were right: you have to learn to get over disappointments."

I hope I haven't laid that one on a bit thick! he thought. But Mr Crustscrubber was obviously taken in by Tony's words.

"You put that very well, Tony!" he praised him. "I think we can be very pleased with the effect that the holiday has had."

"Yes, I agree," said Tony, and in the hope that they would now talk about the strange patient, he turned his gaze on the thick folder that was lying in front of Mr Crustscrubber.

"The treatment course," he began cautiously, "could you try it out on me?"

Mr Crustscrubber smiled – for the first time that evening. And then Tony knew that for Mr Crustscrubber, the routine part of the consultation was now over, and that now at last they could talk about the study course he had developed and its tests . . . on vampires!

Not Afraid of Vampires?

"Try it out on you?" Mr Crustscrubber ran his hand slowly, almost devoutly, over the folder. "Well I could, but you don't suffer from any phobias, in other words, any particularly violent fear of anything. At any rate, your parents haven't let me know of any. On the contrary, they think that you are far too fearless and intrepid!"

"Did they say that?" Tony was flattered.

"And what's more, it's true," agreed Mr Crustscrubber. "After what your parents told me . . . "

"What did they tell you?" asked Tony, growing suspicious.

"That you go wandering about outside even after dark, that you aren't a bit afraid of cemeteries, nor vampires . . . "

Not afraid of vampires? That was the very key-word that Tony had been waiting for!

"But I am!" he objected. "I am afraid of vampires!" Then he added craftily, "For instance, I was afraid of the one that was here with you just now!"

"So you do believe that he really is a vampire?" asked Mr Crustscrubber, studying Tony closely.

Tony nodded. "Yes."

"What makes you think so?"

"The smell."

"The smell?" Mr Crustscrubber's eyes twinkled with amusement.

"I admit, he does smell terribly strongly of lily- of-the-valley and violets. But he could have bought that perfume in any chemist shop."

"No, I wasn't talking about the perfume," said Tony. "It's his own smell, which he's trying to cover up with the perfume."

"His own smell?"

"Yes, his vampire smell!"

"Hmm," said Mr Crustscrubber, and this time he did not look so amused.

"You're right," he said after a pause. "I too have noticed how peculiar it smells in my room, after he has been. Certainly not just of lily-of-the-valley and violets, but of something musty and damp, rather like in a cellar . . . "

"That's the vampire smell!" confirmed Tony. "It's because vampires always have to sleep in their ancient coffins."

"I am very impressed that you know so much about vampires!" remarked Mr Crustscrubber approvingly.

"I know a lot of other things too!" said Tony.

"Do you? What sort of things?" asked Mr Crustscrubber, looking at Tony expectantly.

Tony took a deep breath. "You can recognize them from their pale skin, especially round the rims of their eyes. That's because they can never go out in sunlight."

"Precisely!" exclaimed Mr Crustscrubber.

Tony looked at him in bewilderment.

"That's exactly where my problem lies," Mr Crustscrubber explained. "It's through my course, my de-sensitization course, that I'm hoping they will learn to

expose themselves to the sun's rays."

"Vampires can learn to do that?" For a second, Tony was speechless.

"I haven't got definite proof, at least not yet," answered Mr Crustscrubber. "But I shall find out as soon as I can test the course on a genuine vampire!"

Igno von Rant

"What about the one who was here just now?" asked Tony. "Isn't he a genuine vampire?"

"If only I knew," answered Mr Crustscrubber. "He says that he isn't a vampire. But when we first started the course, he would only come to see me in the evening, after the sun had set."

"And now he's coming before sunset?"

"Yes, about half an hour before. I have tried a couple of times to find out something more precise about him – where he lives, how old he is, where he comes from. But all he says is that his name is Igno von Rant and that he isn't a vampire."

Tony bit his lip so hard with excitement that it hurt. What Mr Crustscrubber had just told him was unbelievable, absolutely sensational – providing that this Igno von Rant was a genuine vampire!

The fact that he claimed *not* to be one proved nothing: it was probably just a safeguard. And after the meeting in the passageway, Tony no longer doubted, in fact he was absolutely certain, that this weird black-haired man was no human – but a vampire!

"I've been racking my brain to come up with a way to find out whether he is a real vampire," Mr Crustscrubber was saying.

"And have you?"

"Well, he's not in the telephone directory, and no one seems to know him either. But there was one thing that began to bother me . . . "

"Bother you? What was that?"

"That over-keen nightwatchman at the cemetery, McRookery! He told a reporter that it was his ambition to create the first vampire-free cemetery in Europe, and that was why he had begun to plough up the old part. At any rate, that's what it said in the newspaper. And that made me prick up my ears, I can tell you!" he went on. "For if my patient, Igno von Rant, really did turn out to be a proper vampire, then I thought he would most likely live in the graveyard. And if this McRookery chap was saying he was determined to create the first vampire-free cemetery in Europe, he must have noticed something in the graveyard – something to reinforce his belief that there actually were vampires there!" Mr Crustscrubber paused. He took a couple of deep breaths before continuing.

"And so, if there really were vampires living in the cemetery, I thought to myself that one of them must be my patient – Igno von Rant! And to stop McRookery driving out my patient, I decided then and there to launch the campaign to 'Save the Old Cemetery'."

He gave a deep sigh.

"Yes indeed, and it was through this campaign that we managed to stop the work on the cemetery."

His Own Coffin

"But perhaps this Igno von Rant doesn't live in the cemetery at all," suggested Tony.

Mr Crustscrubber frowned. "Where else could he live?"

"What about in a cellar?"

"You mean, vampires don't always sleep in graveyards?" asked Mr Crustscrubber in surprise.

"No, vampires can sleep anywhere, as long as it's in their own coffin. That's why they have to take their coffins with them if ever they move."

"His own coffin . . . " Mr Crustscrubber whistled softly through his teeth. "I never thought of that. I could introduce a coffin into my desensitization programme, a real coffin, and see how Igno von Rant reacts."

He scribbled something down excitedly in the file.

"Perhaps that brings me a step forward . . . " he murmured. "I must find out for certain, once and for all, whether or not he is a vampire. Can you give me any further help?" he asked, without looking up.

"Help? In what way?"

Mr Crustscrubber raised his head and looked at Tony with a conspiratorial smile.

"By introducing me to your two strange friends!"

He could only mean Anna and Rudolph! thought Tony. "Why should I introduce you to my friends?" he asked suspiciously.

Mr Crustscrubber laughed. "Don't worry, nothing would happen to them. But your mother has told me so much about black cloaks, pale faces and nocturnal expeditions, that I have simply become rather curious. And your friends might even know a real vampire!"

"What put that idea into your head?"

"Well, if they're always going around dressed in such extraordinary clothes, it could be that a real vampire might have come up to them once – a vampire who . . . " he smirked, "mistook them for real vampires? Don't you think such a thing might have been possible?"

"That a real vampire might have come up to them?" Tony drew down the corner of his mouth doubtfully, so that Mr Crustscrubber would not notice how excited he felt. "And suppose they really did know a vampire," he asked. "What then?"

"Well — " Mr Crustscrubber made an inviting gesture. "Then I would ask that vampire if he would like to take part in my desensitization programme, to rid himself of his fear of sunlight."

Tony was silent, his mind racing. The possibilities that were being opened up here to the vampires were so colossal that he did not know whether to believe in them or to view the whole thing as lunacy. But there on the desk lay the thick file with the course of treatment. And Igno von Rant *was* a vampire, Tony did not doubt that for a moment!

"This course — " he began, but at that moment there was a knock at the door.

Secret Conspirators

"What is it?" called Mr Crustscrubber irritably. The door opened and Mrs Crustscrubber peered into the room.

"Tony's parents have arrived," she said, closing the door again quietly.

Mr Crustscrubber looked at his huge wristwatch. "Oh," he said, "our hour is well and truly up." He stood up.

Tony got up from his chair too, his head swimming and his legs feeling strangely shaky. The things he had just heard from Mr Crustscrubber were so extraordinary, so momentous, that his parents' arrival had taken him completely by surprise. He gulped.

"My friends," he said, "I – I'll ask them whether they know any vampires. And if they do know one, shall I ring you?"

"Yes, good idea!" Mr Crustscrubber opened a drawer in his desk, pulled out a piece of paper and gave it to Tony. "My number's on this." It was the same sheet of paper that Tony had seen in the waiting room.

Please help us preserve the old cemetery . . . For further information, please contact G. Crustscrubber, tel. 481218 read Tony.

"May I take this with me?" he asked.

"Of course! But wait — " Mr Crustscrubber pulled a little red book out of one of his trouser pockets and flicked through it. "I think I may still have an appointment free on Monday. Are you free to come at half-past six?"

Tony nodded. "Sure!" he said, adding to himself. "The pottery class will just have to go by the board." His parents were bound to think that an appointment with Mr Crustscrubber was much more important.

And Tony was right.

His mother certainly looked worried when she heard that Tony was to go back for an appointment with Mr Crustscrubber as early as Monday. And Dad couldn't stop himself from joking, "Tony seems to have a whole heap of problems to sort out!" But he did suggest that he should take Tony on the bus route, so that in future Tony could go to the psychologist on his own without having to change buses.

So far, so good . . .

Even so, Tony could not get to sleep when he lay in bed a short time later.

If what Mr Crustscrubber had told him about the study course with the unpronounceable name was true, then it would be a revolution for the vampires!

He thought of Anna, and how she had dreamed of sitting next to him, just once, in class at school. If the course worked, perhaps she would be able to go to school every day – if she still wanted to!

But it wasn't just school: the vampires could go shopping, to the hairdresser, to the dentist . . . Perhaps, after a while, they would not look so pale any more – they might even get a slight suntan! And then they wouldn't need to be afraid of being recognized as vampires, and persecuted any more! Provided that Mr

Crustscrubber's course of treatment really did have the desired effect. Under those circumstances, Tony thought it might even be quite tempting to be a vampire himself . . .

It would mean that he would have eternal life, and not just that, he would be able to go on living as he had been up till now – though he'd have to make certain changes to his eating habits, but he'd soon get used to them! And then Tony could be with the Little Vampire for always – and with Anna too.

He felt his ears turn red. No, he mustn't think of all that yet! First and foremost, he had to make certain of the main thing – whether the course worked or not.

Mr Crustscrubber and he were now allies in this. No, they were conspirators, secret conspirators! With these thoughts in his mind, Tony finally fell asleep.

With Honey

Even at breakfast the next morning, Tony was still completely under the spell of the conversation he had had with Mr Crustscrubber, and he chewed at his raisin bread without much of an appetite.

"You do seem to be worried about Monday!" his mother observed.

"About Monday?" repeated Tony, looking up from his plate. Had Mr Crustscrubber told her about the study course?

But now she went on to say, "I suppose you're having a test on Monday, and you haven't prepared for it yet!"

"Oh, you mean school!" Tony groaned audibly. "No, there's nothing we're meant to have done." Then he added slyly, "My teacher isn't as mean as *you*!"

Mum retorted indignantly. "What is that supposed to mean?"

"Well, that you probably *do* give everyone a test on the first day back at school!"

"No, I do nothing of the sort!" she retorted. "It was just that from your expression I guessed you must have something unpleasant hanging over you."

"Me? Something unpleasant?" Tony grinned and, thinking of the vampires' Coming Home party on

Sunday, he said, "As long as we stick together, it could be really nice!"

"Stick together indeed!" said his mother sharply. "The best thing would be if they got rid of teachers altogether, and then you pupils would not be disturbed!"

"I'm sure Tony didn't mean it like that," said Dad. "And we ought to be thinking of what we still need to buy. I bet Tony needs some mini cartons of drink for school."

"Yes I do!" said Tony. Then he'd have a couple of presents for tomorrow evening, for Anna.

"And I need bars of chocolate!" he added.

"Bars of chocolate?" repeated Mum, frowning. "I thought we had agreed, that in future you would only take honey-flavoured muesli bars?"

"Ollie's allowed to eat sweets all day."

"Ollie would!" said Mum spitefully.

"Yes, and that's why he's much better than me at football!"

"Football?" said Dad. "I thought you played hockey together!"

"Football *and* hockey."

"Well, at your party next Saturday, there will only be things that are good for you to eat!" said Mum.

"That'll be interesting," sighed Tony.

Dad laughed. "Perhaps we shouldn't be too strict about what they eat, Hilary," he said. "There are bound to be cream cakes and ice-cream and biscuits at Granny and Grandpa's tomorrow – and I'm sure Granny bakes with sugar, not honey!"

"What?" exclaimed Tony. "We're going to Granny and Grandpa's? Not in the evening?"

"Why not?"

"Because — " Tony cleared his throat, "we *have* got

93

some work to do for school." And because he was pretty bad at maths, he added, "A maths test!"